W9-BUM-421

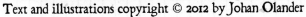

FOR OLIVIA, VIVIENNE,
AND BEATRIX

Text and illustrations copyright © 2012 by Johan Olander

AMAZON PUBLISHING
ATTN: AMAZON CHILDREN'S BOOKS
P.O. BOX 400818
LAS VEGAS, NV 89149
WWW.AMAZON.COM/AMAZONCHILDRENSPUBLISHING

LIBRARY OF CONGRESS CATALOGING-IN-PUBLICATION DATA
Olander, Johan.
My robots : the robotic genius of Lady Regina Bonquers III / by Johan
Olander. — 1st ed.
p. cm.
Summary: Depicts robotic inventions designed by a Scottish recluse and
described in sketchbooks recently found in her abandoned castle.
ISBN 978-0-7614-6173-9 (hardcover) — ISBN 978-0-7614-6174-6 (ebook)
[1. Robots—Fiction. 2. Robotics—Fiction.] I. Title.
PZ7.O4233My 2012
[Fic]—dc23
2011036697

Photo on page 7: "Elaine Hammerstein," Library of Congress, Prints & Photographs
Division, George Grantham Bain collection [reproduction number, LC-DIG-ggbain-33140].
There are no known restrictions on the use of photos from the George Grantham Bain
collection. We apologize for any omission or error in this regard and would be pleased to
make the appropriate acknowledgment in any future printing.

The illustrations are rendered in ink, pencil, watercolor, and oil paint on various papers and
boards. Color additions and enhancements were created with Adobe Photoshop.

BOOK DESIGN BY KRISTEN BRANCH
EDITOR: MARILYN BRIGHAM

Printed in China (W)
First edition
10 9 8 7 6 5 4 3 2 1

MY ROBOTS

THE ROBOTIC GENIUS OF LADY REGINA BONQUERS III

JOHAN OLANDER

AMAZON CHILDREN'S PUBLISHING

DEAR READER,

IT IS WITH GREAT PRIDE AND JOY THAT I PRESENT TO YOU the amazing robotic creations of Lady Regina Bonquers III, who was perhaps the world's greatest robot maker.

At one point in time, Lady Bonquers was almost famous, but after several unfortunate incidents that damaged her reputation, she and her work were more or less forgotten—until two years ago, when a trove of sketchbooks, diaries, and notes was discovered in the attic of her abandoned Scottish castle. They were found by two young relatives, Oscar and Beatrix Bonquers, nine and eleven years old, respectively. The pair immediately realized the importance of these papers but were unable to get the attention of anyone in media or academia. Since they were familiar with my previous scientific work on aliens and monsters, they requested my assistance, which I happily extended to them.

In this volume I have collected the most fascinating robots ever seen and some never before seen. Many of the images in this book are from Regina's personal notebooks and research documents.

During her career, Lady Bonquers created several companies to market her robotic creations. But Regina's business skills were not as strong as her skills in robotics, and things never worked out quite the way she'd hoped.

Bonquers's disappearance occurred decades ago and is still unexplained. On a cold November morning in 1972, a delivery boy, attempting to deliver supplies from the general store in the village of Outatheway, found the castle empty. When he returned to the village, he informed the local police officer, Constable McMadgins.

An investigation followed. McMadgins's report, filed on the twenty-third of November, 1972, states, "No evidence of forced entry or foul play was seen on the premises. The castle appears completely cleaned out; not a trace of the lady of the house or her robotic machines could be found."

Due to the lack of interested parties—Lady Regina's relatives lived far away and hardly knew her—the investigation was soon filed away as "unsolved," and no further actions were taken.

In the international circle of pseudoscientists and mad geniuses, where Lady Bonquers is still remembered, there have been many theories about her disappearance—whispers of secret government conspiracies, robot uprisings, or even alien intervention. But no one truly knows what happened to Lady Regina or her robots.

However, this volume should firmly establish Lady Regina Bonquers III as the unbridled genius she was, or perhaps still is. . . .

Lady Regina Bonquers III as a young woman. This is the only known photograph of her.

Lady Bonquers's deserted castle in Loch MeeAhwey, Scotland

Castle Bonquers

PRIMO MORONE

PRIMO MORONE BECAME LADY BONQUERS'S ASSISTANT in the late 1950s. Most people believed that he was an eccentric Italian engineer who went to Scotland to work for Lady Bonquers because of his love of all things Scottish and robotic.

However, the sensational drawing of Primo on the opposite page makes it abundantly clear that he was, in fact, a robot. Lady Bonquers must have wanted Primo to appear humanlike, since much energy was spent on the detailed mechanics behind his face, as well as on his unique style and elaborate back story.

Primo Morone always wore a kilt and was a regular at the local public house, The Hog's Wallow, in the nearby village of Outatheway. According to some of the old villagers who were acquainted with him, Primo was a man of few words. The owner of the public house, Albert McFingle, seventy-eight, couldn't remember a single time he had heard Primo speak, other than some guttural grunts. McFingle said the grunts sounded sort of like "Thanks," "G'day," "G'd ev'ng," and such, but the same could be said about several other customers, so it was nothing out of the ordinary. Primo was responsible for ordering all of Bonquers's supplies and often spent time in the post office and general store. He was the point of connection between the lady and the village.

Moveable plates allowing for Humming

facial expressions

THIS IMAGE IS THE ONLY RECORD DESCRIBING PRIMO MORONE AS A ROBOT. IT IS FROM ONE OF BONQUERS'S LATEST NOTEBOOKS, DATED BETWEEN JUNE AND NOVEMBER 1972. IN EARLIER NOTEBOOKS, PRIMO IS MENTIONED IN PASSING. FOR EXAMPLE: "PRIMO SECURED 45 KILOS OF URANIUM FOR THE EXPERIMENTAL NUCLEAR REACTOR" AND ". . . DEAR PRIMO IS AN EXCELLENT ASSISTANT, BUT SOMETIMES I WONDER IF HE'S NOT FROM ANOTHER PLANET."

Mrs. Marsh, the owner of the general store, gave me this shopping list which she said Primo handed her in 1971. She had kept it because "there was still a good lot of blank paper left on the sheet."

Mixed with common everyday items are odd amounts and substances.

The volume of sweets—twelve packages of biscuits and 2 kilograms of Turkish delight—is also somewhat out of the ordinary.

2 KG KIPPERS
2 LITERS MILK
2 CANS OF BEANS, WHITE
1 AQUANET HAIRSPRAY
4 KG WHEAT FLOUR
6 CANS OF SARDINES
2 LOAVES OF BREAD
6 LITERS SULPHURIC ACID
1 TUBE OF TOOTHPASTE
2 KG MERCURY
2~3 KG POTATOES
1 KG CARROTS
200 KG ROCK SALT
150 KG LEAD INGOTS
12 PACKAGES MCVITIES BISCU
2 KG TURKISH DELIGHT

SLOBOT

THIS CREATION WAS BASED ON THE INGENIOUS TECHnology of the Slinky toy. Its body was made up of one continous steel spring, and it moved in a snakelike fashion.

The SLOBOT's primary job was to clean sewers. The robot could enter through very narrow pipes, and its powerful jaws and teeth could chew through almost any kind of blockage and break it down into easily flushed slurry. The robot's eyes were also powerful lights, enabling it to find problem areas. Lady Bonquers had several of these robots deployed in her castle's plumbing system and never had any problems. However, one time Primo Morone (see page 8) had heard that a plumbing issue was affecting the whole village of Outatheway. Toilets and drains were backing up. Primo decided to do something about it; he didn't tell anyone before deploying two SLOBOTs into the toilets of the public house.

In a matter of hours, the sewers flowed much better, but a panic had broken out. Villagers reported having seen "alligators" or "monsters" in their toilets and coming out of storm drains on the streets. Suspicions were directed toward Castle Bonquers. But since Lady Regina had no knowledge of Primo's involvement, she emphatically denied having anything to do with it. Nobody asked Primo.

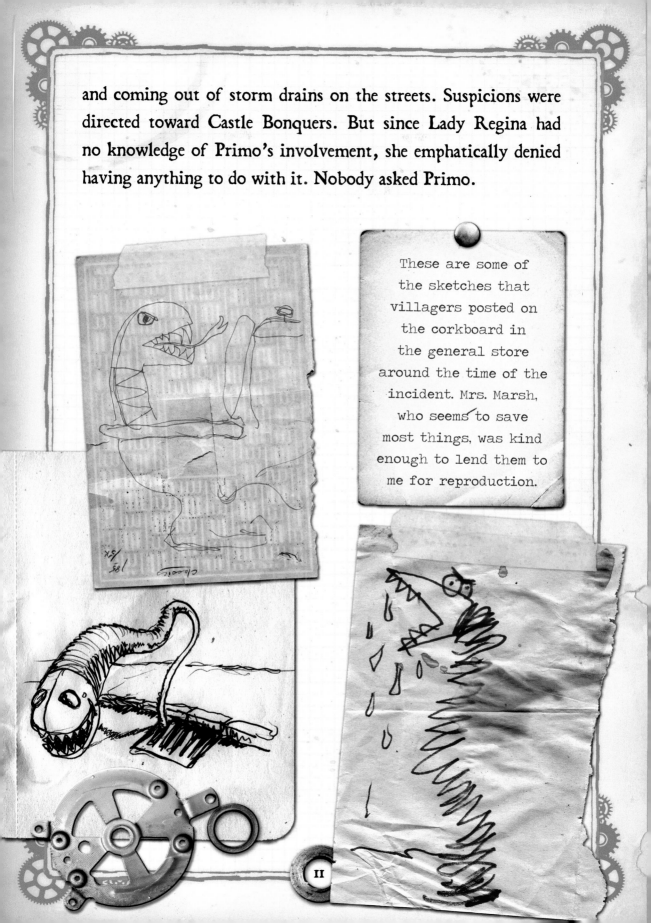

These are some of the sketches that villagers posted on the corkboard in the general store around the time of the incident. Mrs. Marsh, who seems to save most things, was kind enough to lend them to me for reproduction.

EXPLORING FROG

THE EXPLORING FROG WAS A ROBOT VEHICLE DESIGNED to transport humans exploring exotic and harsh environments. Taking its inspiration from nature, the Exploring Frog moved with forceful leaps, just as a real frog does. Some ingenious programming went into the robot's ability to maintain balance while jumping, say from one rock to another while exploring mountains, or when leaping into water from land and vice versa.

The Exploring Frog obeyed spoken commands, and for the passengers who rode inside the machine, it was important to designate a "commander"—one person who spoke the commands to the robot in an assertive way. To avoid confusing the machine, it was best if the other passengers spoke only in hushed voices or in sign language.

The Exploring Frog supposedly had a sophisticated navigation system based on an immense database of maps. However, since this was before the time of GPS satellites, it is a mystery how the Exploring Frog was able to "know" where it was at any given time.

These two illustrations are from the sales brochure.

The Exploring Frog was practical for exploration in harsh conditions, be it underwater, in swamps, in ice and snow, or even on other planets. It seated five humans and maintained a comfortable level of oxygen, temperature, and pressure.

The Frog in arctic exploration mode, equipped with snowshoes

THE FROG-LEAP WAS AN EFFICIENT MODE OF MOVEMENT FOR THE FROG, ESPECIALLY IN DEEP SNOW, IN WATER, AND IN LOW-GRAVITY ENVIRONMENTS. BUT IT HAD THE UNPLEASANT SIDE EFFECT OF CAUSING SEVERE MOTION SICKNESS IN MOST HUMANS; CASES OF NECK INJURIES WERE ALSO REPORTED. ONLY A HANDFUL OF EXPLORING FROGS WERE EVER PRODUCED.

FOR MOTION DISCOMFORT

please place in waste receptacle after use

Bonguers Exploration
IN BUSINESS FOR SCIENCE

A "sick bag" from the Exploring Frog

CHORE MASTER X2000

The Chore Master X2000 was invented in the late 1940s. It served Lady Bonquers well throughout her career. The robot came with a variety of attachments. Whenever Lady Regina needed help around the house, she'd invent a special attachment for the Chore Master for that task.

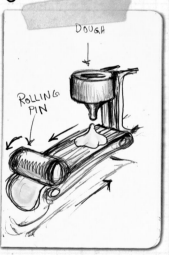

DOUGH

ROLLING PIN

PIZZA ATTACHMENT

The pizza-making attachment of the Chore Master is a good example of how specific this robot's tasks could be. Other specialized chores the robot handled included vacuuming and general cleaning; laundry washing (its "belly" became a washer-dryer), ironing, and folding; as well as painting and light carpentry (fixing things around the castle). There were many food-related attachments and gadgets, such as an ice cream maker, toaster, barbeque, popcorn maker, cotton candy maker, and deep fryer.

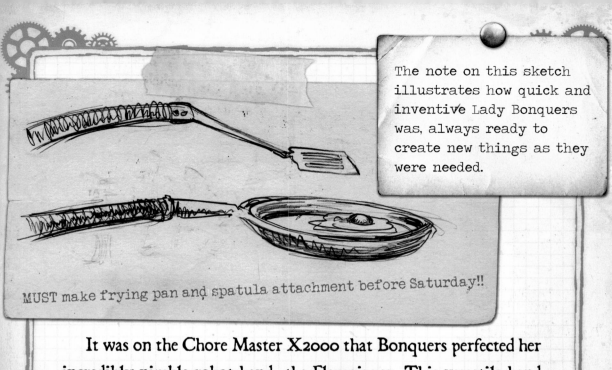

The note on this sketch illustrates how quick and inventive Lady Bonquers was, always ready to create new things as they were needed.

MUST make frying pan and spatula attachment before Saturday!!

It was on the Chore Master X2000 that Bonquers perfected her incredibly nimble robot hand, the Flexgripper. This versatile hand was eventually used on many of her robots.

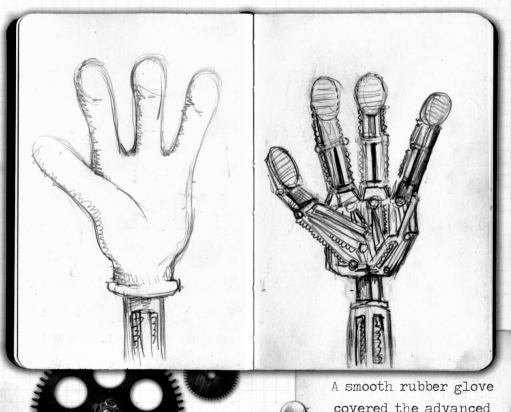

A smooth rubber glove covered the advanced mechanics of the Flexgripper, giving it a humanlike appearance.

The earlier model, Chore Master X1000, depicted in the charred sketch above, was prone to starting fires with its pizza oven attachment.

Before the Chore Master got its final design, Lady Bonquers experimented with another version that she referred to simply as Domestic Bot. Because of its small size and limited reach, Regina abandoned that particular design in favor of the much taller Chore Master. The Domestic Bot became an oversized shoe-shine machine.

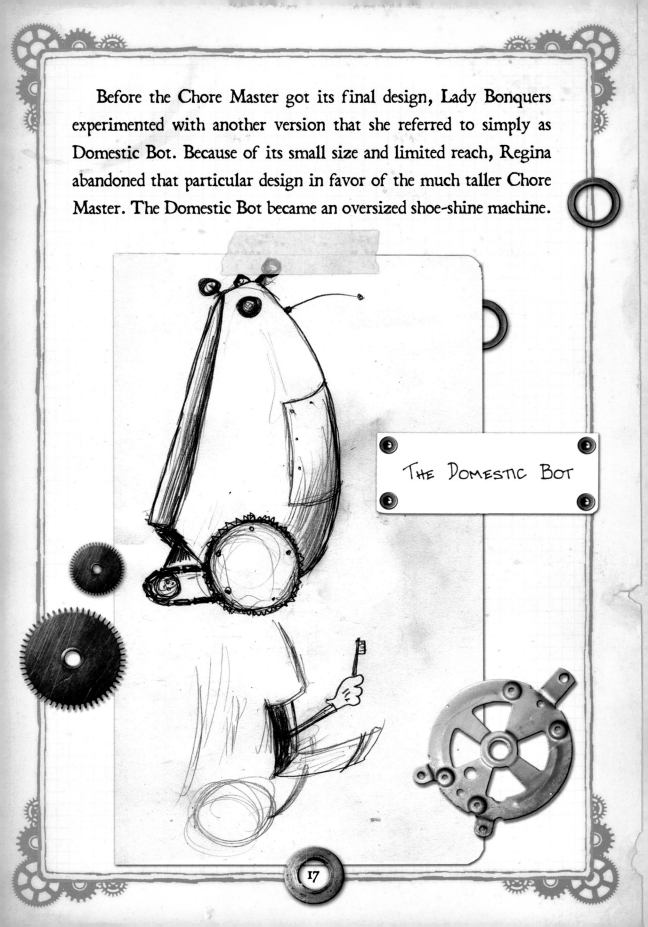

THE DOMESTIC BOT

ODORO 1

THE ODORO-1 WAS ONE OF REGINA'S earliest creations. It was an odor-detecting robot she invented for her personal use. She had always been sensitive to smells and often found herself wasting hours looking for the origins of different stinks. The ODORO-1 was the solution. Bonquers made no real effort to market the ODORO, but she did make some preliminary notes on how she could advertise it.

Have you ever been bothered by a mysterious smell?

This robot will find the source of the stench and allow you to expose it, whatever it happens to be: a polluting factory, stinky brothers, or that fancy imported cheese.

I found this cardboard sheet with scribbles about the ODORO among Lady Regina's notes.

From the sketches of the ODORO-1, we can deduce that there was some kind of radio connection or control involved in the design, but we don't know what function it might have had.

Regina soon realized that the robot wasn't likely to be sold; most people weren't as bothered by smells as she was, and the machine itself sort of stunk. (She had converted a lawnmower engine to run the ODORO, and the gasoline fumes were in many cases worse than the odors which had irritated her in the first place.) It was also pretty loud.

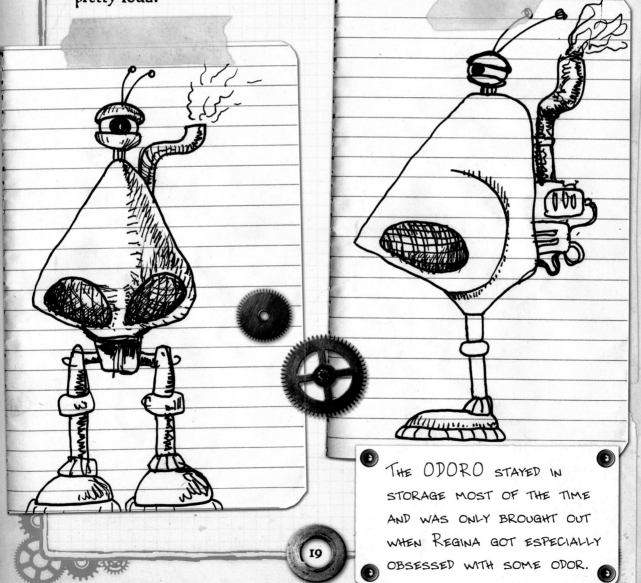

THE ODORO STAYED IN STORAGE MOST OF THE TIME AND WAS ONLY BROUGHT OUT WHEN REGINA GOT ESPECIALLY OBSESSED WITH SOME ODOR.

FIREFIGHTING ROBOT

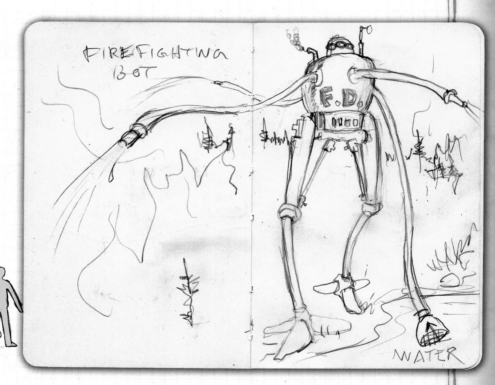

FIREFIGHTING BOT

WATER

The Firefighting Robot was one of the more useful robots to come out of Regina's workshop.

It can be described as a giant mobile pump-and-hose system. The robot could attach itself to fire hydrants or suck water from rivers and lakes and shoot out an impressive amount of water.

But the robot was much more than that. Its hoses were made from Bonquers's patented artificial muscle material, so each hose could move, hold, and lift independently. It also had several different tools, including an axe and chainsaw. But perhaps the most impressive tool was the "plucker." The plucker was a large, gentle hand that could pluck animals and humans out of hazardous situations and place them safely on the ground or into a secure chamber on the rear of its body, which had a closed system of oxygenated air.

The rescue chamber

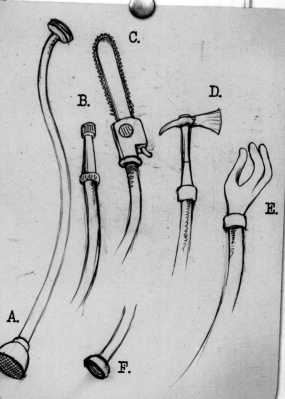

THE TOOLS INCLUDED:
A: SUCTION HOSE, WITH GRIDDED FRONT END FOR SIFTING ROCKS AND OTHER DEBRIS FROM NATURAL WATER SOURCES
B: STANDARD FIREFIGHTING HOSE
C: CHAINSAW
D: AXE
E: PLUCKER
F: SUCTION HOSE WITH FIRE HYDRANT CONNECTION

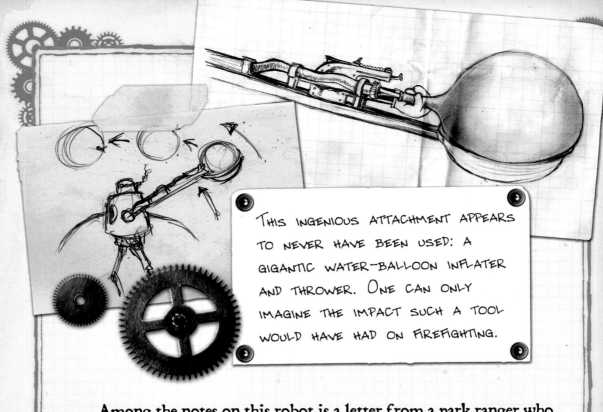

Among the notes on this robot is a letter from a park ranger who was saved by the robot during a large forest fire.

To Lady Regina Bonquers III,

Your robot saved my life. It lifted me out of a shallow pond, where I was stranded, and put me into the chamber in its body. The only problem was that the chamber was already occupied by a cougar, two bear cubs, six squirrels, and a bald eagle. We were all petrified by each others' presence, not to mention being in a state of shock from the fire. But we all squeezed together in the small space, and somehow, the hum of the machinery or perhaps the air within the compartment lulled us all into a deep sleep.

In a copy of Lady Bonquers's reply letter, she explains that yes, indeed, the air contained a natural sleeping agent made from roasted turkey. It was added to the air to prevent dangerous situations in which different species—some prey, some predator—were put into the chamber together.

SAVED BY A ROBOT!

WEE-WOO

A page from the comic magazine *Rescue Ranger*, c. 1954

PERSONAL GROOMING ROBOT #2

(PGR M₂)

THE **PGR M2** WAS A VERY SMALL robot designed to be a pocket-size personal barber. It probably inspired some of today's modern grooming tools. The robot removed unwanted nasal hair conveniently and without pain (at least in theory) and performed other facial grooming duties, such as pimple-popping and eyebrow and ear-hair plucking. It could also apply basic makeup.

The PGR M2 was equipped with a radio receiver and a small speaker to entertain the user with music or talk during the grooming session. It recognized normal speech and obeyed simple commands, as long as they were spoken in a clear voice.

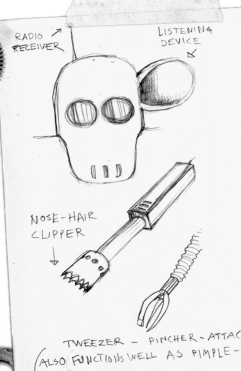

RADIO RECEIVER

LISTENING DEVICE

NOSE-HAIR CLIPPER

TWEEZER - PINCHER - ATTACHMENT (ALSO FUNCTIONS WELL AS PIMPLE-POPPER)

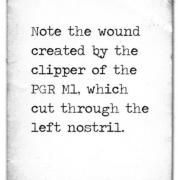

Note the wound created by the clipper of the PGR M1, which cut through the left nostril.

The programming of this sophisticated and miniscule robot was a challenge. Its predecessor, the **PGR M1**, was prone to causing severe injuries. The M2 version had a much less powerful clipper, which could not cut deeper than a few millimeters. However, customers still complained that many of its actions were quite painful, and the **PGR** never became popular.

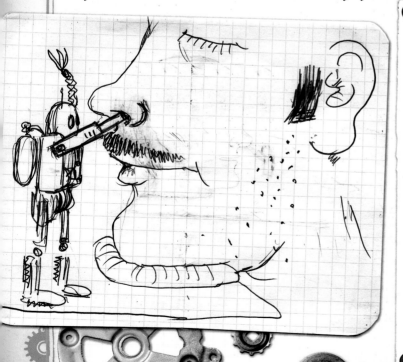

THIS DRAWING FROM THE CONSTRUCTION MANUAL SHOWS THE PGR PERFORMING ITS DUTIES. THE INSTRUCTIONS STATED THAT THE PERSON BEING GROOMED SHOULD GET COMFORTABLE AND REST HIS CHIN ON A SMALL PILLOW OR PIECE OF FOLDED TOWEL ON TOP OF A TABLE. THEN HE WAS TO RELAX AND LET THE PGR DO ITS JOB.

REPLICANT BOT

THE REPLICANT BOT COULD BE USED TO CREATE A replacement for yourself on those occasions when you might want to have an "extra you." The basic robot was completely blank, covered by a flesh-colored, rubbery material. Hundreds of tiny, synchronized projectors displayed images of the user from inside the "skin," thus creating the appearance of a reasonably lifelike substitute.

The interior "body" stretched between 4.5 feet and 6.5 feet, and the skin could be inflated and/or deflated to approximate any body type—from old lady to young boy, from pudgy to lean.

Regina admitted in her research notes that it was unlikely a user would fool parents, siblings, or even teachers in a close-up situation; the technology was just not that good. But the robot could still be very handy in low-light situations and larger gatherings in which the user would be just one in a crowd.

The Replicant was able to interact socially in a limited way. It responded politely to yes and no questions and said a few longer lines that could be preprogrammed based on the type of event it was attending.

For a large family gathering, the user could give it lines such as "Aunt Sophie looks very young" or "This cake is delicious."

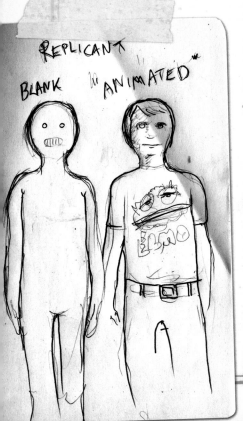

REPLICANT

BLANK   "ANIMATED"

In an educational setting, the user could have it say, "That's really interesting" or "According to some studies, that is correct." The important thing was to provide sentences that didn't invite replies or start conversations, since the robot would be unable to continue the conversation.

The Replicant in action was sometimes described as "very creepy."

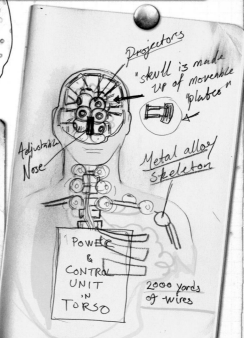

Projectors

"skull is made up of moveable "plates"

Adjustable Nose

Metal alloy Skeleton

1 POWER & CONTROL UNIT IN TORSO

2000 yards of wires

The machinery inside the Replicant was highly complex. However, most of its computing power was spent on creating the illusion of a human. The part left to handle speech and intelligence was little more than the equivalent of the technology in a talking toy.

On one occasion, a Mr. Albert Sneaquy sent a Replicant to a family wedding, and the robot malfunctioned. It overinflated its skin and subsequently popped like a balloon—a very big scandal in the Sneaquy clan. This illustration of the event appeared in the local paper on June 16, 1968.

ENVIRONMENTAL CLEANER ROBOTS

(ECB MODEL TERRA & MODEL AQUA)

BONQUERS WAS A NATURALIST BY NATURE. EVEN IN the late 1940s she was worried about how humans treated the planet. She invented these two robots as a solution to the problem of pollution. She referred to them as "sister robots" since they used essentially the same technology to do the same job, the only difference being that one worked on land and one worked in water.

The water-based model, Aqua, skimmed the surface of rivers, lakes, and oceans, feeding on bottles, wreckage, oil, or any garbage that might be in the water. Terra, the land model, walked along highways and in parks, eating any litter it could find. Both models got their energy from breaking down garbage into useful and/or inert (inactive) substances.

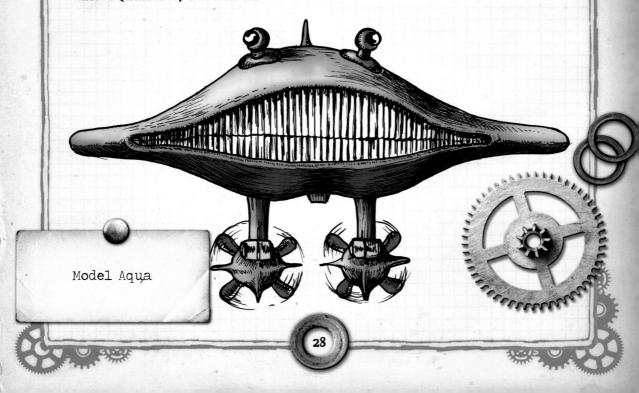

Model Aqua

Model Terra

LITTER
EATER

(PRODUCES A PELLET FERTILIZER)

SKIMMER ROBOT

BONQUERS'S FIRST SKETCHES
OF THE ENVIRONMENTAL
CLEANER ROBOTS

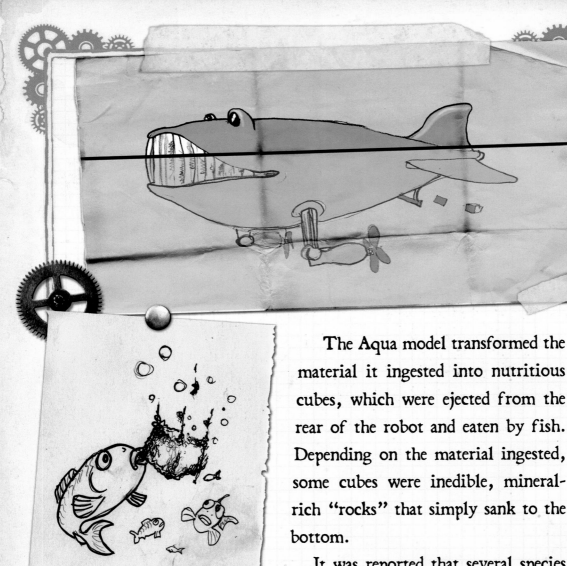

The Aqua model transformed the material it ingested into nutritious cubes, which were ejected from the rear of the robot and eaten by fish. Depending on the material ingested, some cubes were inedible, mineral-rich "rocks" that simply sank to the bottom.

It was reported that several species of fish began to follow the robots. Apparently they loved the taste of the edible cubes.

Model Terra attracted a similar following, but instead of fish, the Terra was followed by human mineral hunters. In urban areas, the robot would often consume discarded radios or other electronic trash, and the resulting "nuggets" would contain high concentrations of valuable metals. But most of the Terra's cubes were made up of a pasty substance that fertilized plants and was enjoyed by birds.

CROCOBOT COMPACTOR

The Crocobot Compactor was another of Lady Bonquers's inventions meant to help humans deal with the environment in a better way. Like the smaller Environmental Cleaner Robots (see pages 28 and 29), the Crocobot was designed to find trash and transform it into either reusable material or inert substances. Forty feet tall, the robot handled such objects as discarded vehicles and even small houses. Bonquers hoped the Crocobot would be helpful after natural disasters as well as in day-to-day operations at junkyards.

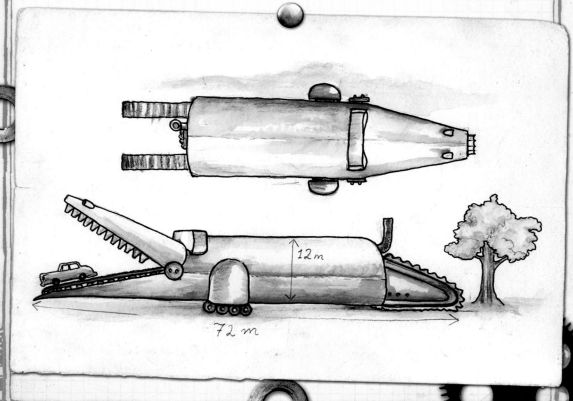

12 m

72 m

A wrecked car could come out of the Crocobot as the following: several lengths of steel rods; a cube of solid glass; cubes of clean, reusable plastic and rubber; a large ball of yarn; 1 to 10 quarts of oil; and a handful of inert rocks.

Each Crocobot Compactor came with two Auxiliary Support Crocobotinis (ASCs for short), which organized the processed materials coming out of the Crocobot. When not in use, the Crocobotinis traveled in the belly of the Crocobot.

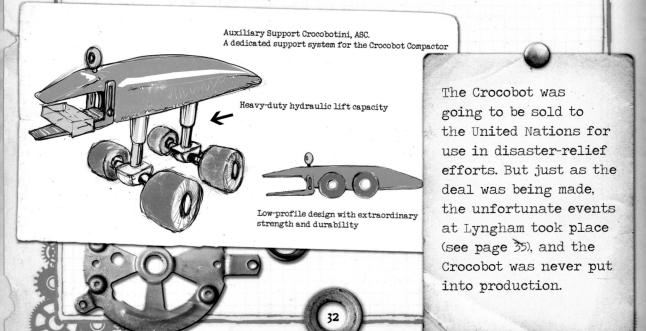

Auxiliary Support Crocobotini, ASC.
A dedicated support system for the Crocobot Compactor

Heavy-duty hydraulic lift capacity

Low-profile design with extraordinary strength and durability

The Crocobot was going to be sold to the United Nations for use in disaster-relief efforts. But just as the deal was being made, the unfortunate events at Lyngham took place (see page 35), and the Crocobot was never put into production.

RO-BULANCE

A ROBOT MEDIC

THE RO-BULANCE WAS SUPPOSED to become the ultimate helper in an emergency, acting as an ambulance and medic rolled into one. The robot had an encyclopedic knowledge of human injuries and how to fix them. It could run fast and simultaneously treat patients. The robot could also be sent into dangerous areas where human medics could not go. Unfortunately, the RO-BULANCE was very clumsy. Regina's one prototype actually fell into Loch MeeAhwey and was never seen again. This is how she described what happened:

"RO-BULANCE"
For emergency services, especially where human medics might be in danger.

Emergency Medical supplies

Protective "Awnings"

Gurney

The infernal machine couldn't walk in a straight line. I tried reprogramming it several times, but it would always trip or bump into something. After days of working on its gyroscopic sensor, I thought I had fixed it and took it outside the castle. As soon as I let it go, it walked a straight line! So straight, in fact, that it went right into the lake and kept walking. I could see it for a while until it got too deep.

The RO-BULANCE could have become a great tool for emergency services, but Regina gave up on it after the mishap at the loch.

THE BUILD-O-BOT

(B.O.B.)

At one point in time, Lady Bonquers created a robot she hoped would revolutionize the construction industry. The Build-O-Bot 200 was billed as the ultimate tool for all construction needs.

The 250 was the B.O.B. equipped with wrecking balls instead of the 200's tools and gripping arms, and it was programmed to destroy

360° Vision

B

200

B.O.B. 200 & 250

B.O.B. the Build-O-Bot 200 and 250 *The most versatile construction machines you'll ever buy!*

THE ULTIMATE TOOL

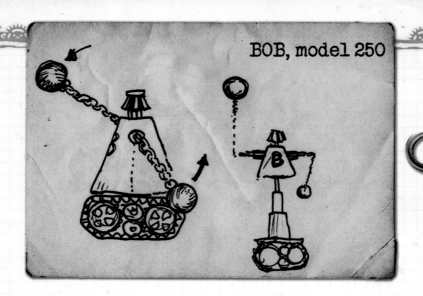

BOB, model 250

buildings or anything else in need of demolishing. It could wreck "a three-story brick building in less than twenty minutes, creating easily carted debris," according to the sales brochure.

In 1963, a large construction firm bought four B.O.B.s—two model 200s and two model 250s. Shortly after, the programming of the 250 somehow "infected" the 200s, probably through their shared charging station. When the 200s were turned on for the following day's work, they went berserk, wrecking everything in their way. In a last-ditch effort to save the town of Lyngham, Scotland (population 12,000), Bonquers programmed the 250s to battle the 200s.

The Destruction of Lyngham

All four robots were reduced to "easily carted debris," as was a large portion of the town.

Bonquers's reputation was irreparably tarnished. No more B.O.B.s were ever built. And it was Lady Regina's last attempt at commercializing her robots.

INTERPLANETARY AUTONOMOUS BATTLE-BOT

(IPABB)

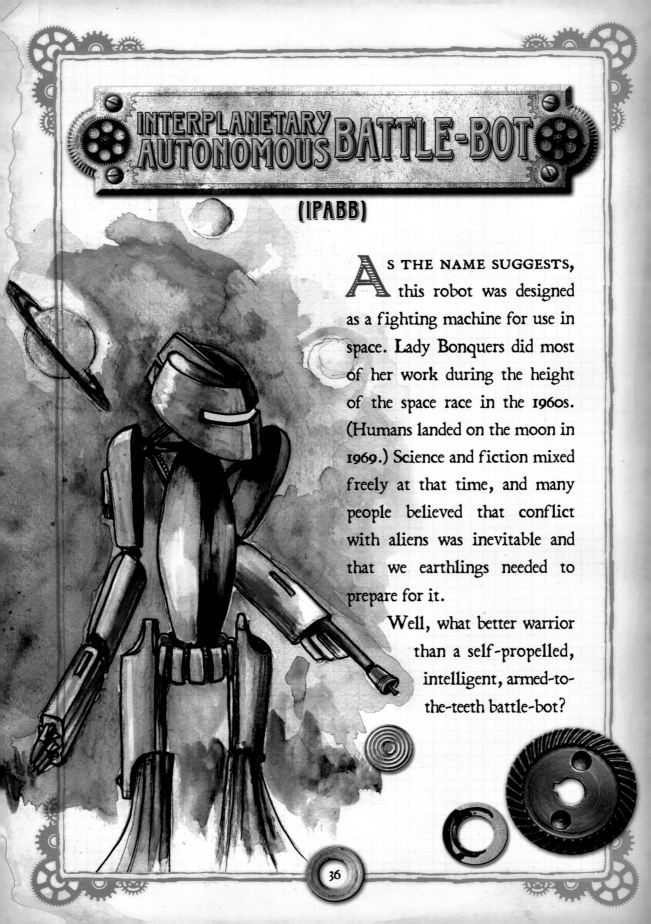

AS THE NAME SUGGESTS, this robot was designed as a fighting machine for use in space. Lady Bonquers did most of her work during the height of the space race in the 1960s. (Humans landed on the moon in 1969.) Science and fiction mixed freely at that time, and many people believed that conflict with aliens was inevitable and that we earthlings needed to prepare for it.

Well, what better warrior than a self-propelled, intelligent, armed-to-the-teeth battle-bot?

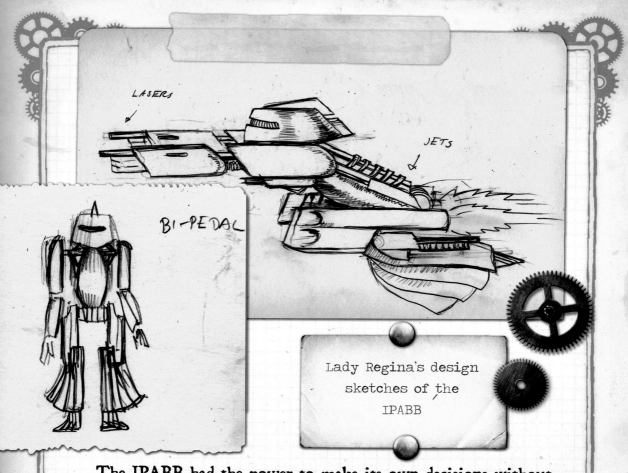

LASERS

JETS

BI-PEDAL

Lady Regina's design
sketches of the
IPABB

The IPABB had the power to make its own decisions without human involvement. The programming that went into creating its "brain" was based on the idea of curiosity as the foundation for intelligence.

However, Bonquers's ingenious formula for intelligence backfired. Curiosity turned out to be *too good* of a formula; the robots soon figured out that they didn't want to be fighting machines. The idea of fighting aliens on faraway planets was not appealing. Instead, their curious "minds" led them into the fields of science and art.

Only four IPABB units were built. They took human names: Ed, Will, Fiona, and Jill. (Lady Bonquers did not assign a "he" or "she" to the IPABBs; they chose the distinctions themselves.)

Jill turned out to be a talented sculptor. Ed and Will formed a musical duo that produced strange modern music. Fiona worked for several years as Bonquers's assistant. Because of her unique ability to interface directly with computers in the lab, Fiona became a brilliant computer programmer; she was responsible for creating the "brains" of several of Bonquers's later robots.

Alive!

New sculptures celebrating life
by

Jill

Jill's sculptures were shown in a few galleries. This is an invite for one of her shows. She often used discarded machine parts and weapons as well as living plants in her pieces. The piece in the invite is called Laughing Car-Hood With Orchids, Bamboo, Pumpkins, and Bomb.

FIONA, IN THE LAB

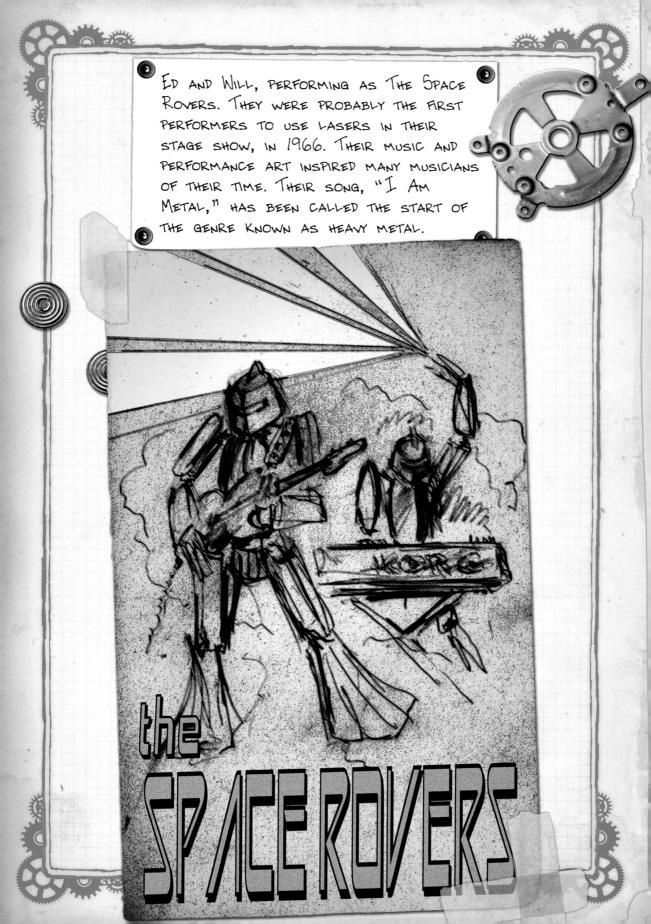

ED AND WILL, PERFORMING AS THE SPACE ROVERS. THEY WERE PROBABLY THE FIRST PERFORMERS TO USE LASERS IN THEIR STAGE SHOW, IN 1966. THEIR MUSIC AND PERFORMANCE ART INSPIRED MANY MUSICIANS OF THEIR TIME. THEIR SONG, "I AM METAL," HAS BEEN CALLED THE START OF THE GENRE KNOWN AS HEAVY METAL.

the
SPACE ROVERS

AUTO CLOWN

"THE AUTO CLOWN IS THE SUPREME ENTERTAINER. It will always find a way to brighten your day!" Those are the first lines in a brochure that Lady Regina was drafting for the Auto Clown. The brochure stated that the robot came programmed with jokes for all ages, magic tricks, juggling skills, the ability to make a full range of animals and objects from balloons, as well as two thousand balloons and an air compressor.

The robot also employed a virtually endless array of physical comedy tricks, such as tripping and falling in forty-seven different ways, seventeen ways of falling off a chair, eight ways of falling off a ladder, and much more. It came equipped for pie making (and throwing) and could also play several musical instruments while riding a unicycle.

Introducing
the

AUTO
CLOWN

Bonquers Entertainment
IN BUSINESS FOR FUN

Despite having three legs, the Auto Clown was able to ride a unicycle, as shown in this drawing from Lady Regina's notebooks.

Soap Bubbles

Air

Water

spins

loud-speakers

Very large "pants" conceal a large variety of props

pie

Banana peel

Bonquers's drawing of the Auto Clown, with detailed design notes. Air, bubbles, and water came out of nozzles in its fingertips.

Looking at the brochure, it's clear that Bonquers planned to start a service in which her Auto Clown robots could be rented for birthday parties and other events. However, as with most of Lady Regina's commercial plans, it didn't work out. Her first (and last) client for the Auto Clown was disappointed when the robot apparently made endless fart-noises with balloons at his birthday party and then began heckling the guests.

See below the exasperated letter of complaint from the client, twelve-year-old Angus McFarthing (who, one might suspect from his name, probably was very sensitive to jokes about flatulence).

Your clown robot was not funny! It was annoying! No matter what commands my father and I tried, it kept making the most horrible noises with balloons. In fact, I think the robot was trying to be mean on purpose! We demand a full refund!

In Regina's notes, she deduced that the error was, in fact, an actual "mean streak" in the programming, which she was unable to explain. The returned robot stayed with her in the castle. It supposedly taunted everyone who visited with mean-spirited jokes, until finally Lady Regina recycled its parts to build the Babysitter Bot (see page 43).

Primo Morone (see page 8) made a watercolor painting of the Auto Clown in its later years. One can sense its meanness.

BABYSITTER BOT

THE BABYSITTER BOT WAS ONE OF the last inventions known to have been created by Bonquers. It was, as previously men-tioned, made up of parts recycled from the Auto Clown (see page 40). The computer "brain" of the Babysitter Bot was completely rebuilt, and the mysterious mean streak that had made the Auto Clown a failure was eliminated.

According to Bonquers's notes about the Babysitter, Fiona (the IPABB, see page 38) did some of her best programming work on this robot. The Babysitter Bot had a brain programmed to mimic the developmental stages of human babies. It could be set to enjoy the same things as a one year old or a five year old. When deploying the robot, the user could reset the program so everything seemed brand-new and fascinating to the robot, even though it might have, for instance, bounced a ball against a wall or listened to the same knock-knock joke for hundreds of hours.

The Babysitter Bot's task was not merely to be a friend to human babies but also to be a responsible babysitter. It had a whole second brain that monitored the actions of both baby and robot.

When needed, the second brain directed the robot to slow play so that the baby would settle down for naps. The robot could gently rock the baby with a bottle and perform the general tasks of a parent or babysitter. It was able to do everything from diaper changes to feedings to reading bedtime stories. It came fully loaded with a complete library of children's literature and all existing lullabies written by December 1971.

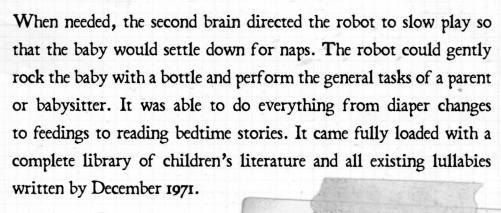

Two studies of the
Babysitter Bot
in action

BONQUERS CREATED THE
BABYSITTER BOT FOR HER
NIECE ESMERALDA BONQUERS,
THE MOTHER OF OSCAR AND
BEATRIX BONQUERS.

DRESSER ROBOT

(JACQUES)

T HE DRESSER ROBOT— always referred to as Jacques in Bonquers's notebooks—was designed to be her personal groomer and fashion consultant. It was responsible for decisions regarding clothing, hairstyles, and accessories. Its most important task was to read several international fashion magazines to keep its on-board database up-to-date on the latest fashions. As Lady Bonquers's personal inclination was to not care at all about fashion, she created Jacques so that she could maintain a fashionable appearance for business meetings and other excursions outside the castle.

It became apparent to her that she needed help after a humiliating incident in 1965, which is described in a newspaper clipping taped into her notebook.

BLOW-DRYER ↓

45

Lady Bonquers Causes Commotion at Conference

By Alphonse Alliterate

Copenhagen, Denmark. Lady Regina Bonquers III, the eccentric but brilliant robotics genius, was prevented from entering the conference halls of the Annual Robot Conference in Copenhagen yesterday. Apparently her appearance was so disheveled that the security guards at the door mistook her for a vagrant and denied her entrance.

She loudly exclaimed, "I am Lady Regina Bonquers the third. Make way, you fools!" Due to the language barrier, the guards thought she was saying that she was "bonkers" and subsequently questioned her sanity, which drove Lady Bonquers to respond in even harsher terms. A scuffle ensued, and Lady Bonquers was escorted off the grounds for a psychiatric evaluation.

According to eyewitness accounts, she was dressed in a stained lab coat, one green Wellington boot, and one orange clog. Her hair was tied in a large knot on her head, described as "resembling a crow's nest," and was held together by four yellow pencils and a metal ruler.

Double Dipping Dolphins

By Alphonse Alliterate

Miami, Florida. A pair of dolphins in captivity near Islamorada in the Florida Keys have bee...

Jacques's arms could employ several different attachments. In hairstyling mode, one hand could be a blow-dryer and the other a comb or scissors; or both arms could be equipped with versions of the Flexgripper (see page 15).

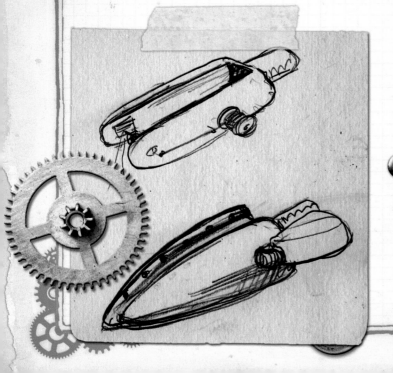

There were also some highly specialized attachments, such as the steamer iron and sewing machine.

In his spare time, Jacques enjoyed making paper dolls. Lady Regina dressed very conservatively, so perhaps the paper dolls were Jacques's only arena for bolder fashion statements. Clearly he was a very sophisticated robot.

CRUSHING CATERPILLAR & SNOUTED SENSERS

(EXCAVATING ROBOT 2-3P WITH DUAL CONTROL UNIT 2-PP & 2-PQ)

THE CRUSHING CATERPILLAR AND SNOUTED SENSERS robot was an excavation and mining machine capable of tunneling for approximately 12 meters per day. A belt took rocks from the mouth of the machine through processing stations within its body. The robot ejected gravel-size pebbles from the rear.

The Caterpillar was a clumsy machine that basically just crushed rocks all day. What made the robot truly valuable, though, were the control units designed to work with it. Each Caterpillar came with a pair of Snouted Sensers that could detect valuable rocks, ore, and crystals or steer the Caterpillar in the correct direction for simple excavation projects. The units were in constant contact with the Caterpillar through radio waves. In essence, the Sensers were the Caterpillar's brain and sensors.

A 2-PQ unit in a cheerful pose

The snout of the Sensers was packed with technology that allowed them to "sniff out" all kinds of minerals. They were able to toot loud warning signals as well as transmit focused radio waves.

According to Bonquers's notes, there was a very curious and inexplicable glitch in the programming of the Sensers. Every night after they completed their tasks, they'd start dancing. They would choreograph elaborate routines and perform for hours. They used their snouts to play jazzy horn music. Lady Regina was very amused by their behavior.

One of Bonquers's sketches of the Sensers performing a show

The Sensors could walk on walls and ceilings with their technologically advanced feet, an ability that was often prominently displayed in their dance routines.

The Crushing Caterpillar was used to dig beneath Bonquers's castle. In the later years, most of Lady Regina's robots were made in these new underground facilities.

When Bonquers's relatives visited the castle years after her disappearance, they found the underground area completely flooded.

To the Castle

Storage

Repairs

To assembly

A WATERCOLOR SKETCH BY PRIMO MORONE (PAGE 8) OF LADY BONQUERS'S UNDERGROUND FACILITIES AS THEY APPEARED WHEN IN USE

EXTERMINATOR ROBOT
(XT 300)

CASTLE BONQUERS HAD a rodent problem. Rats and mice loved the castle almost as much as Lady Regina did. She was constantly at war with them. The Exterminator Robot was her ultimate response. It was about the size of a cat (Bonquers was allergic to cats) and performed its mouse- and rat-hunting tasks with a determination that even a ferocious cat would envy.

The robot's energy came from breaking down its prey within its chemical "stomach," similar to the way animals and humans get their energy. If the robot didn't catch prey, it would shut off. The machine was programmed to dislike getting shut off, so it was always motivated to be on the hunt.

The robot was covered with a "skin" that could be changed.

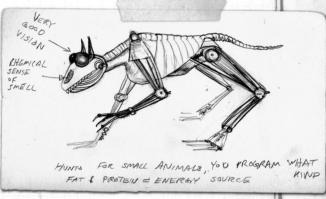

VERY GOOD VISION

CHEMICAL SENSE OF SMELL

HUNTS FOR SMALL ANIMALS, YOU PROGRAM WHAT KIND
FAT & PROTEIN = ENERGY SOURCE

Camouflage skin for inside the castle

Camouflage skin for outside use

Camouflage skin for outside use during winter

PERSONAL PORTER & TRANSPORT ROBOT

(PPTR M70)

GO! ~ anywhere

PPTR M70

Personal Porter and Transport Robot
Model -70

Your intelligent, capable, and safe travel aid

Bonquers Exploration
IN BUSINESS FOR SCIENCE

The PPTR M70, or "Poppy" as the model also became known, was another attempt by Lady Bonquers to achieve financial success from her robots. Printed marketing materials were made, and ads were taken out in travel magazines.

Lady Bonquers thought the robot would be a must-have item for world travelers. She based this idea on the fact that she personally disliked travel, especially carrying cumbersome, heavy suitcases. In her mind, the PPTR solved this problem. Unfortunately, folks had already started to experiment with putting wheels on suitcases, and that, combined with little need for robotic porters among the general public, sealed the PPTR's fate. That you could "go anywhere," even in water, with the PPTR was not enough of an added value; people found cars and boats quite convenient and comfortable.

Another image from the marketing materials, showing how the PPTR could traverse bodies of water with the help of "duck feet" mounted on its "ankles" and an inflatable floatation device that came out of its rear compartment

A safe, dry ride even in water with the optional "duck feet"

Just ask for: PPTR-M70 A# D-X2

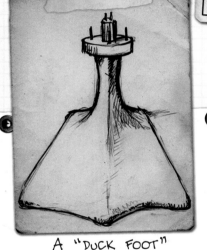

A "DUCK FOOT" ATTACHMENT

Four units were sold to an Australian ostrich farmer who claimed the PPTR was the perfect tool for herding birds. He maintained the robots until the late 1980s, when they were sold as scrap to a junkyard in Brisbane.

Regina mentioned the Australian ostrich rancher in her diary and made this lively sketch.

SATELLITE VIDEO EXPLORER 1

(SAVE-1)

BE-SM-1A

SPACE MISSION 1A
1965
Bonquers Exploration
IN BUSINESS FOR SCIENCE

MUCH OF LADY BONQUERS's career took place during the heyday of the space race, and she was clearly interested in sending her robots to space.

She joined the race in early 1965 with the launch of Bonquers Explorations's first space mission: BE-SM-1A. In a way, she was ahead of her time since most people just wanted to shoot a monkey or a human into space and get him back to Earth safely. Lady Regina wanted to find valuable information about Earth from space. The Satellite Video Explorer 1 launched from a location near Castle Bonquers. The fact that Bonquers Exploration, Regina's company, could launch a satellite of its own was big news at the time.

The SAVE-1 was meant to keep an eye on weather, natural disasters, and unrest on Earth. It had superpowerful telephoto lenses behind its "eyes" and was able to monitor large areas of Earth. Video was sent to Earth via transmitters in the machine's core.

The only problem was that the robot reported *everything* as a disaster. A rainy day was reported as "WEATHER ALERT! WEATHER ALERT! Massive rains cover large portions of the northern hemisphere! STAY INSIDE!!"

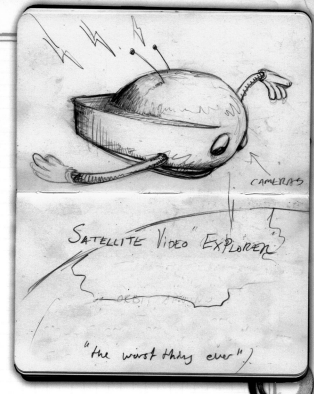

When a minor volcano (one that had been active for as long as anyone could remember) erupted on Iceland, it was reported as "ALERT! ALERT! IMMINENT DANGER. PART OF EARTH EXPLODING!!" Meanwhile, the actual footage showed a small puff of steam coming out of the volcano, only slightly bigger than the normal everyday steam puff.

The alarmist reports became so annoying that Regina was forced to shut down the SAVE-1's transmissions. What had started out as a big success for Bonquers Exploration turned into another commercial failure.

The SAVE-1 was mocked by the media at the time. This cartoon, cut from an unknown publication, was found among Lady Regina's notes.

As far as I know, the SAVE-1 is still orbiting Earth, most likely aghast at what it sees.

INTERPLANETARY ROVING SAMPLER ROBOT

(INPROV-SR)

L IKE THE IPABB (SEE PAGE 36), the INPROV-SR was a robot designed for space. It was created to travel to unexplored planets in space to pick up all kinds of samples. The INPROV-SR was equipped with six arms, two of which had Flexgrippers (see page 15); the remaining arms could be fitted with a variety of instruments—everything from pincers to the "small animal net mitten" to the "vacuum-suction-nozzle and sample bag."

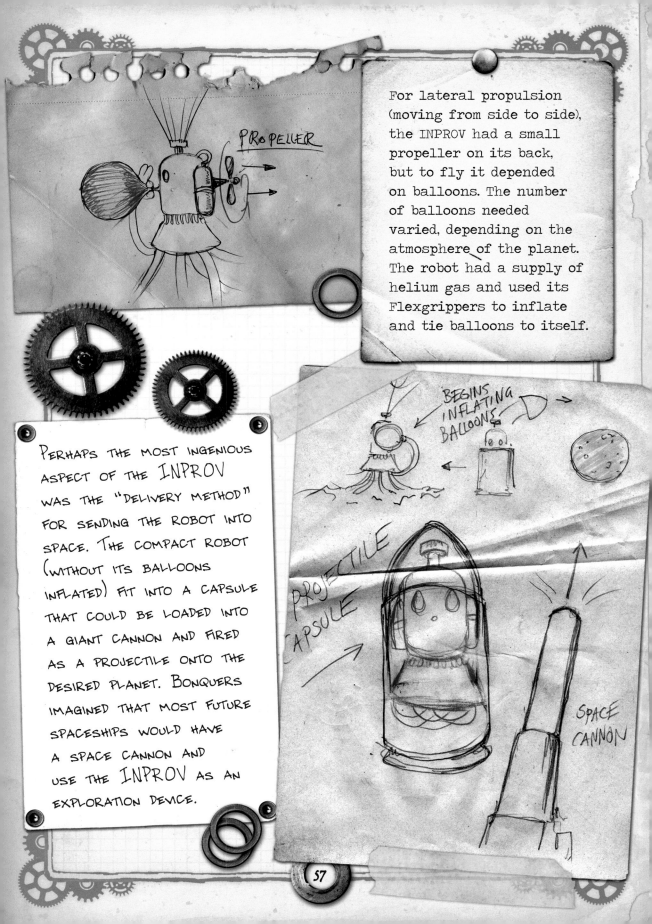

PROPELLER

For lateral propulsion (moving from side to side), the INPROV had a small propeller on its back, but to fly it depended on balloons. The number of balloons needed varied, depending on the atmosphere of the planet. The robot had a supply of helium gas and used its Flexgrippers to inflate and tie balloons to itself.

PERHAPS THE MOST INGENIOUS ASPECT OF THE INPROV WAS THE "DELIVERY METHOD" FOR SENDING THE ROBOT INTO SPACE. THE COMPACT ROBOT (WITHOUT ITS BALLOONS INFLATED) FIT INTO A CAPSULE THAT COULD BE LOADED INTO A GIANT CANNON AND FIRED AS A PROJECTILE ONTO THE DESIRED PLANET. BONQUERS IMAGINED THAT MOST FUTURE SPACESHIPS WOULD HAVE A SPACE CANNON AND USE THE INPROV AS AN EXPLORATION DEVICE.

BEGINS INFLATING BALLOONS

PROJECTILE CAPSULE

SPACE CANNON

FINDER

(RETRIEVING ROBOT XI)

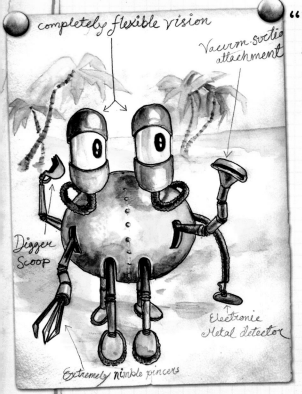

completely flexible vision

Vacurm-suctio attachment

Digger Scoop

Electronic Metal detector

Extremely nimble pincers

"**F**ROM LOST KEYS AND MISSING** toys to pirate treasures, this robot will help you find anything!" That was how Lady Bonquers described the Finder in its sales brochure. The Retrieving Robot was programmed with the most advanced "stuff-finding algorithms" and equipped with state-of-the-art tools.

One of the most fascinating features of this robot was its incredibly flexible "eyes." Strong cables attached the eyes to the main body; they were made of expanding and contracting steel springs that gave each eye independent movement and the ability to see in any direction. (This same technology was later used to create the Firefighting Robot's flexible and strong hoses/arms.)

According to Lady Regina's notes, the independent movement of the eyes sometimes led to a troubling malfunction:

When one eye is looking upside-down and the other is looking in a different direction, it is very difficult for the Finder to balance itself. I will try to adjust its gyroscopic equilibrium to prevent the somersaulting that occurs when this happens.

In other words, the rotund robot would fall into a roll when the eyes were in specific, opposite positions. One can easily imagine the kind of trouble to which this could lead on mountainous terrain.

This illustrates the dangers of imbalance in the mountains. It was published in the trade journal *Treasure Hunter's International Gazette*, Issue #4, April 1967, in which a Mr. Curmudge wrote a mocking review of the Finder, calling it, among other things, an "avalanche of junk."

THE FINDER HAD A VARIETY OF SPECIAL ACCESSORIES, INCLUDING:

- METAL DETECTOR
- POKER, FOR POKING AND SPEARING STUFF
- SIFTER, HANDY FOR RETRIEVING SMALL THINGS FROM SAND, DIRT, OR LIQUIDS
- DRAGGING HOOK, FOR SEARCHING LONG STRETCHES OF SAND, DIRT, OR LIQUIDS
- POWERFUL VACUUM SUCKER, WITH THE SUCKING POWER OF SEVENTEEN EVERYDAY HOUSEHOLD VACUUMS
- DIGGER, A SMALL BUT VERY EFFICIENT TOOL FOR "NORMAL" TREASURE RETRIEVAL (I.E., DIGGING FOR TREASURE CHESTS)
- SEVERAL DIFFERENT PINCERS CAPABLE OF GRABBING ITEMS AS FINE AS HUMAN HAIRS AND AS HEAVY AS LARGE CHESTS AND EVEN SARCOPHAGI

SIFTER

DRAGGING HOOK

SAFE-KEEPING COMPARTMENT

METAL DETECTOR

POKING SPEAR

Very useful when treasure hunting

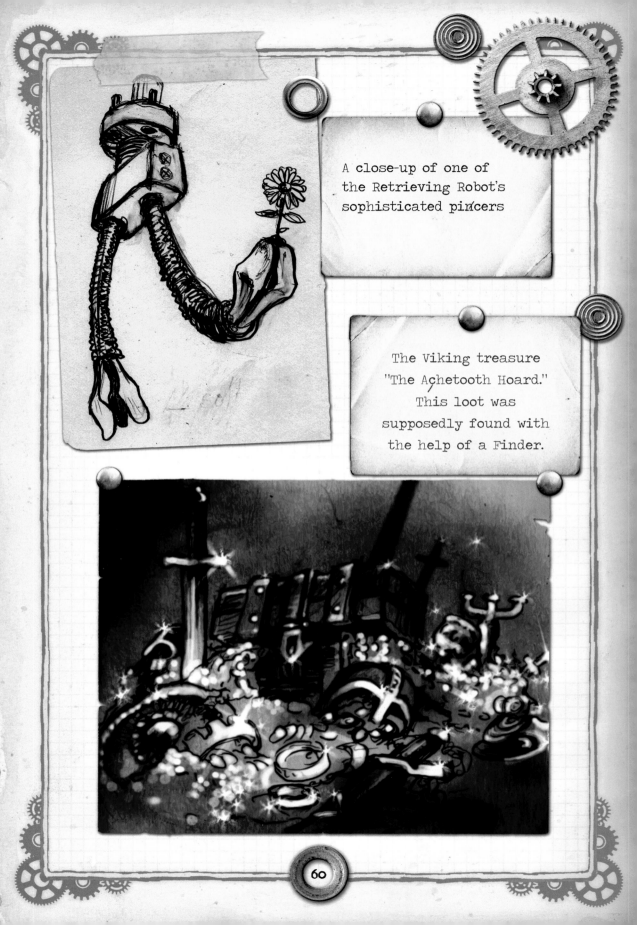

A close-up of one of
the Retrieving Robot's
sophisticated pincers

The Viking treasure
"The Achetooth Hoard."
This loot was
supposedly found with
the help of a Finder.

JABARI

(THE HUGGING ROBOT)

Jabari was named after a dear friend of Lady Bonquers's—her very favorite teddy bear when she was a child. Jabari was designed to be a comfort robot—a hugger. His soft and cozy body was constructed in a similar way to the Replicant's (see page 26); the exterior was an inflatable layer of rubbery material that could be adjusted to varying softness. Jabari's "skin" was also covered in a thick layer of soft synthetic fur.

Jabari was one of a kind—no copies were ever built. Regina's notebooks included just one descriptive entry on this robot, along with a sketch of the robot's mechanicals and a loving portrait done in pencil.

In her notes, it's obvious that Lady Bonquers was very fond of this robot, yet also a bit embarrassed about what could be perceived by others as her childishness.

I found myself longing for the gentle care that my dear Jabari lavished on me as an infant. Nowhere in my life today could I find that assured comfort. So I decided to build myself a hugger, my own childish dream of a giant Jabari, a Jabari who could hug me back and sing simple, comforting songs . . .

JABARI

The Jabari was a large robot that stood more than 7 feet tall.

MAR -- 2013

ON

CASE DANGER

3.5.43
1.443
6.986

PSI

6.47